Meet

Belle

Meet Belle!

Belle comes from a small village
in France. She was raised by
her father, a kindly inventor
named Maurice. The villagers
think Belle is unusual because
she is always reading.

Where is this magnificent castle?

On the other side of the forest from Belle's village.

The forest is very thick.
It is easy to get lost there
if you're not careful.

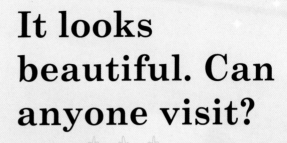

It looks beautiful. Can anyone visit?

No! It is strictly private property.

The owner of the castle does not welcome any uninvited guests.

Who is the owner of the castle?

A scary-looking Beast.

The Beast has Belle's father locked up
in the dungeon at his castle.

Why is the Beast keeping Maurice prisoner?

As a punishment. The Beast was angry when Maurice entered his castle after getting lost in the forest.

What is the Beast's secret?

He was once a human prince. A portrait in the castle shows how he looked before he turned into the Beast.

Who made those slash marks on the portrait?

The Beast. He slashed the portrait in anger. It reminded him of how his life used to be.

Why did the prince turn into the Beast?

An enchantress cast a spell on him. She turned him into a Beast to teach him a lesson about love and kindness.

What did the prince do that was unkind?

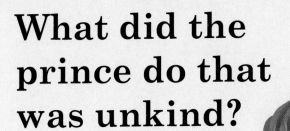

He refused to help an elderly woman. He did not know she was an enchantress in disguise!

Can the spell be broken?

Yes, but there is only one way. The Beast must find someone to love him before the last petal falls from a cursed rose.

Where did the rose come from?

✦ ✦ ✦

The enchantress gave it to the Beast. He keeps it in a secret room in the west wing of the castle.

Why is Belle going to the castle?

She wants to save her father.

Maurice is old and frail. Belle has agreed to take his place as the Beast's prisoner.

How long will Belle have to stay in the castle?

Forever! The Beast has made her promise to stay in the castle all her life. In return he will set her father free.

Who does Belle meet in the castle?

Enchanted objects. The enchantress also cast a spell on the castle's servants. She turned them into objects that can move around and talk!

What do the enchanted objects do?

They look after the Beast and his castle. Cogsworth the clock is scared of getting into trouble with the Beast. Lumière the candelabra enjoys breaking the rules!

Where does Belle sleep in the castle?

In her own large bedroom.

It has a gold four-poster bed with
a beautiful quilt and pillows.

Does Belle like her room?

She likes it better than the dungeon! But she would much rather be at home with her father.

Where does Belle get her yellow gown?

In the Wardrobe. The friendly Wardrobe offers Belle a lot of dresses and accessories to choose from.

Does Belle like having all these new things?

Not at first. Belle was perfectly happy in her old simple dress. However, she does come to appreciate her new things.

Do the enchanted objects welcome Belle?

Yes! They are thrilled to meet her. They hope she will fall in love with the Beast so the spell will be broken.

Is that the only reason they are nice to Belle?

No! They like her and try to cheer her up. Lumière and the feather duster even do a dance to make Belle smile.

Who organizes food and drinks in the castle?

Mrs. Potts the housekeeper.

The motherly teapot whizzes here, there, and everywhere on her food cart.

Mrs. Potts always has a teacup by her side. Who is it?

It's her little son, Chip. Chip gets his name from the tiny chip in his rim. His nose is a cup handle.

Does Belle have nice things to eat?

Every meal is delicious!

In the afternoon there is tea, cake, and juices. In the evening there is a grand feast.

Is the table setting always so fancy?

Yes. The Beast insists on the finest tableware. The table is always set with beautiful crystal serving dishes and gold goblets.

Who keeps the kitchen neat?

The pots, plates, cups, and cutlery! They are all enchanted. They put themselves away after each meal.

Who does all of the cooking?

Chef Bouche. The castle chef takes his job very seriously. There is a lot of cooking to be done to make sure everyone is fed!

What can the Beast see from his balcony?

Anyone approaching his castle.

The Beast keeps a lookout from his balcony for any unwanted visitors.

Why is the Beast worried about visitors?

✦ ✦ ✦

Some people want to harm him.

Many of the villagers have listened to rumors
that the Beast is dangerous.

Is Belle afraid
of the Beast?

Only at first. She soon learns that his beastly looks hide a kind heart. Kindness always beats beauty!

Does Belle ever think about her old life?

All the time. Although she has grown fond of the Beast, Belle misses her father and she is still very homesick.

What is the grandest room in the castle?

✧ ✧ ✧

The spectacular ballroom!

It has polished floors and a gleaming crystal chandelier hanging from the ceiling.

Is the Beast a good dancer?

He is an excellent dancer.

When Belle dances with the Beast, she is amazed at how graceful he is.

Does the Beast mind being a Beast?

✦ ✦ ✦

It makes him very unhappy.

He thinks that nobody could ever love him because of his scary appearance.

Why is Belle not allowed in the west wing of the castle?

The Beast has secret things there. It is where he keeps the enchanted rose and other reminders of his old life.

Does the Beast talk to the enchanted objects?

He often confides in them.

They give him advice about winning Belle's
love. When they do, he listens.

Where does the Beast go when he is sad?

He goes to his parlor. A cup of tea, a comfy armchair, and a crackling fire usually cheer him up.

What is Belle's favorite room in the castle?

The library. There are hundreds of books in the library. Belle wants to read them all!

Does the Beast think Belle is strange for being a bookworm?

✦ ✦ ✦

Not at all. Unlike the villagers, the Beast thinks reading is a perfectly good hobby.

What is the castle like in winter?

✦ ✦ ✦

It is really beautiful. Snow settles on the turrets and covers the trees and lawns outside.

Is there ice skating?

✧ ✧ ✧

No, but there is snow fighting.

Belle throws snowballs as hard as she can.
She may not be as strong as the Beast, but she
still lands some good hits!

What is Belle looking at in that mirror?

The face of her father. The Beast has given Belle a magic mirror so she can see how Maurice is doing.

Is Belle happy to see Maurice?

✧ ✦ ✧

No, she is sad because Maurice looks ill. The Beast cannot bear to see Belle so upset. He sets her free to go to Maurice.

Do Belle and the Beast ever meet again?

Very soon. When Belle hears that the villagers might harm the Beast, she rushes to his side. She loves him too much to stay away!

Is the enchantress's spell broken?

Yes! When Belle says "I love you" to the Beast, the spell is broken and he turns back into a prince.

Is Belle surprised to see the prince?

✦ ✦ ✦

Of course! But when he explains about the rose and the spell, she understands.

What happens to the castle servants?

✦ ✦ ✦

They all return to normal.

The love that Belle and the prince share has broken the spell over the whole castle.

Do Belle and the prince live in the castle?

Yes. It will always be their home. The castle is now a happy place, where visitors are welcome.

What is that picture over the castle gate?

A stained-glass window. It shows Belle and the prince dancing together as they live happily ever after!

Test your knowledge!

1. Where is the Beast's castle?
a) Through a thick forest
b) On a desert island
c) Below a waterfall

2. Why do the villagers think that Belle is different?
a) She only wears green dresses
b) She is always reading
c) She is friendly with teapots

3. Does the Beast like having visitors at the castle?
Yes—he just loves entertaining guests.
No—he does not want anyone inside his castle.

4. Who put a curse on the Beast?
a) An enchantress
b) A wizard
c) A talking frog

5. What is the name of Mrs. Potts' young cup?

a) Scratch

b) Nick

c) Chip

6. Where does the Beast keep the enchanted rose?

a) The west wing of the castle

b) The north wing of the castle

c) The castle dungeon

7. Is the ballroom Belle's favorite room in the castle?

Yes—she loves to dance

No—nothing can beat the library

8. Where does Belle see her father's face?

a) In a magic time machine

b) In a magic tunnel

c) In a magic mirror

Glossary

Bookworm

A person who really
likes reading

Candelabra

A candle holder with
branches

Chandelier

A large, hanging light

Cursed

Someone who is under
a spell

Dungeon

Castle prison cell

Enchantress

A woman who uses magic
to put people under spells

Frail

Weak

Homesick

Longing for one's home

Inventor

A person who creates or
designs something new

Portrait

Painting of a person

Rejects

Says no

Rumors

Stories or reports that
may or may not be true

Turrets

Small towers on top
of a castle

Index

DK Penguin Random House

Project Editor Lisa Stock
Senior Designer Lauren Adams
Senior Production Controller
Lloyd Robertson
Senior Production Editor
Jennifer Murray
Managing Editor Paula Regan
Managing Art Editor Jo Connor
Art Director Lisa Lanzarini
Publisher Julie Ferris
Publishing Director Mark Searle

Written by Tori Kosara
Designed for DK by Elena Jarmoskaite

DK would like to thank Randi K. Sørensen,
Heidi K. Jensen, Paul Hansford, Martin
Leighton Lindhardt at the LEGO Group,
and Chelsea Alon at Disney. Thanks also to
Tali Stock for editorial assistance and
Lori Hand for proofreading.

First American Edition, 2021
Published in the United States by
DK Publishing
1450 Broadway, Suite 801, New York,
NY 10018

Page design copyright © 2021 Dorling
Kindersley Limited. DK, a Division of Penguin
Random House LLC
21 22 23 24 25 10 9 8 7 6 5 4 3 2 1
001-321868-May/2021

Manufactured by Dorling Kindersley
One Embassy Gardens, 8 Viaduct Gardens,
London SW11 7BW, under license from the
LEGO group.

Published in Great Britain by Dorling
Kindersley Limited.

A catalog record for this book
is available from the Library of Congress.
ISBN 978-0-7440-2856-0

DK books are available at special discounts
when purchased in bulk for sales promotions,
premiums, fund-raising, or educational use.
For details, contact: DK Publishing Special
Markets, 1450 Broadway, Suite 801,
New York, NY 10018
SpecialSales@dk.com

Printed and bound in China

For the curious
www.dk.com

MIX
Paper from
responsible sources
FSC™ C018179

This paper is made from
Forest Stewardship Council™
certified paper—one small
step in DK's commitment
to a sustainable future